Natalie

School's First Day of Me

Other titles in the That's Nat Series

Natalie

School's First Day of Me

Dandi Daley Mackall

ZONDER**kidz**

ZONDERVAN.com/
AUTHORTRACKER
follow your favorite authors

We want to hear from you. Please send your comments about this book
to us in care of zreview@zondervan.com.

To Brooks

ZONDERKIDZ

School's First Day of Me
Copyright © 2009 by Dandi Daley Mackall
Illustrations © 2009 by Lys Blakeslee

Requests for information should be addressed to:

Zonderkidz, *Grand Rapids, Michigan* 49530

Library of Congress Cataloging-in-Publication Data

Mackall, Dandi Daley

  Natalie : school's first day of me / by Dandi Daley Mackall.
      p. cm. —(That's Nat!)
  Summary: Five-year-old Natalie worries about all the terrible things that could
happen on her first day of kindergarten.
      ISBN 978-0-310-71568-9 (softcover)
  [1. First day of school—Fiction. 2. Kindergarten—Fiction. 3. Schools—Fiction. 4.
Friendship—Fiction. 5. Fear—Fiction. 6. Christian life—Fiction.] I. Title.
  PZ7.M1905Np 2009
  [Fic]—dc22   2008049740

Editor: Betsy Flikkema
Art direction and design: Merit Alderink

Printed in the United States of America

---

13 14 15 16 17 /QG/ 19 18 17 16 15 14 13 12 11 10 9 8 7 6

Table of Contents

Chapter 1

Big Fat Deal!

My name is Natalie 24 (twenty-four is my favorite number). And I am very much excited on account of in only one week, I am going to be a schoolgirl and go to kindie-garden. That's what!

When I think about going to *real* school, my heart gets thumpy.

Real school happens in a giant big building with a gazillion kids in there. And those kids go to a lunch-room and a gym.

I have already gone to sorta schools. Like Sunday school that is in our church. Plus also, preschool, which happens only some of the days. And not the whole entire day, like real school. And little-kid schools like day care and Mommy's Day Out.

And day camp. Only nobody camps there. And nobody will make a campfire no matter how many times you ask them to.

So you might could think it's not so much of a big fat deal going to a *real* school that goes by the name of Kindie-Garden.

But you would be wrong. It is a very big deal.

And you get new shoes.

"Laurie, why do they call it *kindie-garden* if there's not a garden in that place?" I know there isn't any garden in that real school 'cause my mommy and my daddy took me there on an explore. We saw classrooms and restrooms and a lunchroom. But not one garden.

I am asking this question at the same time I am swinging on my swing in my backyard.

My bestest friend, Laurie, is on the swing next to me. Her swing goes up when mine goes back. And back when mine goes up. Laurie knows about kindie-garden 'cause she has big sisters who already went to that place.

"I don't know why they call it that, Nat," Laurie answers. "I'm just really, really glad we both got the same teacher."

"Me too!" I wanted more than anything to share a teacher with my bestest friend, Laurie. When they told us who we got for teachers and Laurie and I got the same one, I yelled all over the place. Only we were in that special explore meeting with all the parents and kids. And I got in trouble for that yelling.

"What's our teacher's name?" I ask Laurie, on account of I forgot already.

"Miss Hines," Laurie answers.

I practice saying that name. "Miss Hines. I think Miss Hines is very smart. She wears glasses."

"Miss Hines is the nice teacher," Laurie explains when our swings pass each other. "Mrs. Swindler is scary. That's who Sarah had."

Sarah is one of Laurie's big sisters. She knows stuff about everything. Plus also, she wears lipstick.

Laurie drags her foot on the ground so her swing matches mine. We go up together. And back together. Only then it stops working.

Laurie jumps off her swing.

I jump off my swing. Only my swing is up too much high. I'm too far from the ground. My feet land, but the rest of me keeps going. I *crash* hard on my knees and hands.

Laurie comes running up to me. "Nat, are you okay?"

I very much like that Laurie looks scared about me landing hard. "Yeah," I say. I stand up. I really am okay, except for my knees.

Laurie sits on the grass next to me. We have on shorts. Only hers are pink, and mine are purple. She brushes dirt off my knees. "I can't believe summer's

almost over," Laurie says.

I haven't thought about this on account of it's really hot still. But if Laurie says summer is almost over, I believe her.

We sit without talking.

Percy, my fuzzy white cat, walks up and rubs against my leg.

"I love summer," I say.

This is a true thing. Summer is when you do swimming and baseball and playing outside and swinging with your bestest friend, who goes by the name of Laurie. That's what.

And this could make it a sad thing that summer is over.

Only not this time.

On account of I, Natalie 24, am about to go with my very bestest friend to a school that goes by the name of Kindie-Garden.

Chapter 2

Schoolgirls in a Van

"Natalie! Laurie!" my mommy yells at us in the backyard. "Laurie's mother is here."

Laurie and I hop off the ground and race to the front of my house.

Laurie's mom is driving their big golden van. Next to her is Laurie's big sister Brianna. She has curly hair like Laurie's, only brown where Laurie's is blonde.

Laurie's even bigger sister, Sarah, is sitting in the middle of the van.

"Hurry up, Laurie!" Brianna yells out the van window. "There won't be any Nikes left in my size." Sometimes Brianna is not so nice as Sarah. She is never as nice as my bestest friend, Laurie.

My mommy is already talking to Laurie's mom. "Going shopping, Marge?" she asks.

"'Fraid so," says Laurie's mom. "You should come with us, Kelly. One-Stop is having some terrific sales."

Brianna makes a noise like air going out of a balloon. My mommy makes that noise when she is aggravated, which is what other moms call angry.

"Hmmm," Mommy says. "I do have to get new shoes for Natalie before school starts."

"On account of I'm going to kindie-garden," I add. "Can we go with them?" I ask. "Please?"

"Why not?" Mommy answers.

And there are no answers to why not.

Laurie grabs my hand. "Let's get in." She slides open the middle van door.

"I should get your kindergarten list, Nat," Mommy says.

"Yes!" I shout.

At that explore meeting, they gave us a whole page of stuff we need. Like scissors and markers and glue.

Laurie and I climb into the van and find our seat belts.

"I have dance class in an hour, you know," Brianna tells her mom, who is also Laurie's mommy. And Sarah's.

13

"I forgot," Laurie's mom says. "I can't shop very long, Kelly. I'll have to drive Brianna to dance class."

"I'll take *my* car," Mommy says.

"Can I go with *them please*?" I beg.

"Okay by me," Laurie's mom says.

Brianna makes her balloon noise again.

Sarah turns the page of her magazine. I can see lipstick-wearing girls in there. Plus also, some boys. That's what.

"I'll get the list and meet you there," Mommy says. Then she says just to me, "Be good."

Laurie's mom drives regular fast to the store. My mommy catches us in Buddy. That's what I named our car, and my daddy says that is the perfect car name. I wave out the back window at Mommy and Buddy.

"Maybe I can get purple shoes," I tell Laurie.

"That's so cool!" Laurie says. "We got my shoes last week, but they're white. Except they have purple lines on them."

"I love purple lines!" I tell her. Only I don't love that so much as purple-everything shoes.

It is very much fun riding in a golden van. We are all schoolgirls in this place. Except Laurie's mom. "What are *you* getting at the school store, Sarah?" I ask.

Sarah finally looks up from her magazine. "Lip-

stick." She smiles at me. And guess what. She has
lipstick on her teeth.

Laurie giggles. That makes me giggle. And that
makes her giggle.

"So what's with the giggle boxes?" Laurie's mom
asks from the driver's chair.

That makes us giggle more. And I don't even know
why. We giggle like silly until Laurie hollers, "Hey!
That's our school!"

I look outside the window, and Laurie is right. That
big giant building with bricks for walls and sidewalks
and a silvery flagpole is our school, West Side Elementary.

"I really like our West Side Elementary School," I
say to Laurie.

"Well, you can have it," Brianna says back. "I hate
that school."

"Brianna!" Laurie's mom says. "Don't tell them that."

"It's true," she says. "I'm just glad this is my last year there."

"Bri is in fifth grade," Laurie tells me. "Her class is the oldest one in our school." She looks at Sarah, who is tearing out a page of her magazine. "Sarah is in ninth grade."

"Freshman," Sarah says, not looking at her sisters. "I'm a freshman in high school. Next year I'll drive myself to school."

"In that car you plan on winning in the lottery?" her mom asks.

Sarah says something back, but I'm not listening to them.

I am still staring at the back of Brianna's head. "Why do you hate our school?" I ask her.

"Because the teachers are mean," Brianna says.

"Brianna, stop it!" shouts Laurie's mother. She turns the van into the store parking lot.

"Not Miss Hines," I say, remembering that Laurie said we got the nice teacher.

"Whatever," Brianna says. "Wait till you get to know dear Principal Fritz, though. She's a piece of work."

16

"Enough, Brianna," says her mom. "I mean it."

Laurie looks at me kinda scared. Then she turns to Sarah. "*You* liked our school. Right, Sarah?"

Sarah closes her magazine and sets it on the floor. Then she says, "Too many little kids."

Laurie and I make frowny faces at each other.

"And homework," Brianna adds.

I never thought about homework. Or any work. My stomach feels twitchy in a not-so-good way.

Laurie's mom shuts up her van. "Sit tight for a second." She gets out and waves my mom over to us.

Brianna turns around and stares at Laurie and me. "Do you kids even know how to read?"

I shake my head in the no way.

Laurie shakes her head in the no way.

"Too bad," Brianna says.

"Why?" Laurie asks. This is what I was going to ask if I could have gotten those words out. But my neck is kinda chokey.

"Lots of kids starting kindergarten can read these days," Brianna says. "So you guys are already behind."

"But don't we learn to read there?" I ask. My words sound funny 'cause they had to shove past the chokey in my neck.

I glance down at Sarah's magazine. And now I am

seeing what's there besides those lipstick girls.

There are words all over that magazine. That's what.

I stare at those words. I know my letters. Except sometimes the little letters. But not words.

And this is a for-true thing I didn't think about before right now: I, Natalie 24, can't read.

Chapter 3

One-Stop

"Over here!" Laurie's mom shouts outside the van. My mommy drives up and parks Buddy next to us. Sarah slides out of the van and heads for the store.

But Laurie and I keep sitting.

"What's wrong with you two?" Mommy asks, leaning into the van. "Aren't you excited about getting your first-day-of-kindergarten outfits?"

Laurie's mom sticks her head inside the van too. They look like a two-headed mommy. But we don't giggle.

"Brianna, what did you say to the girls?" asks Laurie's mom.

Brianna makes her balloon noise and gets out of the van.

"Don't believe anything she said about kindergarten," Laurie's mom warns us. "You girls are going to love it! Kelly and I loved school."

My mommy unsnaps my seat belt. "Totally!" she says. "Who wouldn't love kindergarten? You have friends there, like Jason and Bethany. And Laurie!"

This is a true thing. I'll see my bestest friend every day for all day.

"After your first day of kindergarten, you girls won't even want to come home," Laurie's mom says.

"But we can't read," Laurie says. "Nat and I are already behind."

Our mommies look at each other. I think they are swallowing laughs. "Is that what Bri told you?" asks Laurie's mom.

Laurie nods.

"That's crazy," Mommy says. "Why do you think they invented kindergarten? So they could teach you to read. You wouldn't want your teacher to feel like nobody needed her, right?"

"*We* need her," I say.

"You girls know exactly what you're supposed to know to enter kindergarten," Mommy says. "You are definitely not behind."

My mom is very smart, and I think I believe her. "Really?" I ask, just to be sure.

"Absolutely!" Mommy says.

"I wish *I* could go to kindergarten again," Laurie's mom says.

"Me too," Mommy agrees.

This idea makes me a little smiley. On account of

I'm thinking our mommies wouldn't fit in those little desks.

"Do you really think Nat and I will like kindergarten?" Laurie asks. But she is already taking off her seat belt.

"No," Mommy says. "You'll *love* kindergarten!"

"'Cause kindergarten is fun?" I ask, trying hard to say that word like Laurie says it. I scooch to the door of the van. "And not boring?"

"Kindergarten rocks!" Laurie's mom shouts.

"And," my mom adds, like a cheerleading girl, "do you know one reason why kindergarten rocks?"

I shake my head in the no way. But I am already thinking of some reasons kindergarten rocks. Like having my own desk. And like Laurie being there every day.

"I'll tell you why kindergarten rocks. New shoes! That's what!" Mommy lifts me out of the van and twirls me around. Then she does the same thing to Laurie.

My mom is so smiley-faced that it's rubbing off on Laurie and me.

Laurie giggles.

Plus also, I giggle.

We are two giggle boxes all over again.

Only as we run into the One-Stop store, there is a tiny bit of chokey still in me.

Chapter 4

Purple Shoes

There are a hundred gazillion people inside this store. Laurie and I stay with our moms. Brianna and Sarah go off all by themselves.

"I like this skirt!" Laurie shouts. She holds up a skirt that would be jeans if it had legs in it.

"Me too!" I shout back. I like real jeans better. But this is the first day of real school.

A gazillion kids are lined up for the trying-on room. So Laurie and I try on these skirts over our shorts right out in front of everybody. This makes us giggly.

"Mine fits!" Laurie shouts.

"Me too!" I shout.

We get to buy these skirts that look alike. I love getting the same skirt as my bestest friend.

Our tops end up different, which is an okay thing on account of mine is purple.

Laurie's mom gets her a white top 'cause it goes with other stuff. I am very glad that in my house, purple goes with everything.

"We are going to be twin schoolgirls!" I shout.

"Twin schoolgirls forever!" Laurie shouts back.

"Next stop, shoes," Mommy says.

"Purple shoes?" I ask.

Before Mommy answers, Laurie grabs my hand. We run down the whole entire aisle to get to that shoe street.

We peek into every shoe box. Then I see shoes sticking out of the wall. "Purple!" I cry.

We race to that shoe wall. There's only one purple shoe on that wall. I hold that shoe over my head and run back up the aisle to find Mommy.

Mommy is coming down the aisle at me. "Natalie, stop running."

I try. "Look! A purple shoe! Can we see if they got two of these shoes around here?"

Mommy takes that shoe and stares at it. "Nat, this is a ladies' shoe."

"I am supposed to act like a lady," I remind her. "Especially in kindergarten."

"It's way too big for you, honey," Mommy says.

"Maybe they have little ones. And I'll get bigger," I promise.

Mommy turns the shoe over and looks at the numbers on the bottom of the shoe. "Whoa! Talk about bigger! Natalie, these shoes cost eighty-five dollars. Put it back where you got it."

I carry the beautiful purple shoe in front of me and walk back to the shoe wall. But I can't get it back up.

So the shoe guy takes it from me.

"Too big?" he asks.

I nod. "You got any little purple shoes?" I ask.

My mom comes up behind me and takes my hand. "Come on, Natalie. We're hitting the clearance racks."

"My mom always goes to those," Laurie says. She holds my other hand.

We walk to the back of the store. There is a big sign over these shelves. Maybe the words say, "Purple shoes here!" Or maybe not. 'Cause I don't know what those words say.

On account of I can't read. That's what.

Laurie and I look at all the shoes. They are not purple.

"These have purple stripes," Laurie says, holding up some very white shoes. "They're pretty, Nat. And my shoes have stripes too. We got them last week right here."

Mommy checks the bottom of those shoes. "Right size. Right price," she says. "How about it, Nat? Why don't you try them on?"

I plop on the floor and try those shoes on my feet.

They have sticky-to-itself tops and no shoelaces you have to tie. And even though they are not purple, my heart gets a little thumpy.

"They're gorgeous!" Laurie shouts.

"Try them out, Natalie. Walk around in them." Mommy points to the back aisle.

I start walking. *Squeak, squeak, squeak,* go these shoes. I very like that squeaky noise. So I make it more, and faster.

Then the shoes start running. Then, they turn around and run even more.

"Natalie! Enough!" Mommy cries.

I slow down those shoes. "Can I wear them home?" I ask.

Mommy shakes her head, but she is smiley-faced. I think she likes my new fast shoes also.

We buy more stuff. Only some of the stuff is boring, like socks.

Brianna cries when her mom won't get her jeans like everybody in her whole class wears. She cries again when her mom won't get her a teeny-tiny red shirt like everybody who is anybody will be wearing. But she gets a bunch of other stuff.

Sarah buys six lipsticks with her own money.

Laurie and I pick out our pencils and markers and

paper. And this is more fun than you think it's going to be.

The last thing Laurie and I get is the very best of all. Except maybe it's tied with getting new shoes. And that is . . . backpacks! Plus also, they are purple. That's what.

When we leave the store, Laurie climbs into the van. But I have to go with my mom in Buddy. And that's okay 'cause that's where my new shoes are going.

Mommy starts up Buddy. I keep holding my backpack. Plus, a bag with markers and glue and pencils in it. Every box of school stuff has words all over it. My backpack has a word on the bottom and a big tag with lots of words. I stare at those words. And I wonder.

"We are twin-backpack schoolgirls!" Laurie shouts out her van window.

I push my window button and shout out of Buddy's window, "We are twin-purple-backpack schoolgirls forever!"

And that feels like a good thing. With only a little bit of chokey in it.

Chapter 5

HyKlas

"What's that sign say?" I ask Mommy.

"No Left Turn," Mommy answers.

We are driving to the grocery store that goes by the name of HyKlas. I never saw all of these signs with words before. Now they are all over the place. Even on cars.

"What's that sign say?" I ask more.

"Buy Now. Pay Later," Mommy reads.

I am thinking about all the things I'd like to buy now. Like a computer. And a purple house. Plus a magic reading machine.

"Buy now and don't pay till later," I say. "That sounds like a very good idea."

"Not so much," Mommy says.

"What's *that* sign say?" I point to a noisy green car that whizzes past us.

Mommy laughs a little. "Honk if you love Jesus," she says.

"Why didn't you honk?" I ask. My mommy loves Jesus. Me too.

"Well," she begins, like she's thinking about this, "somebody else might have thought I was honking at *them* instead."

This is a true thing. I always think honks are for me and Mommy and Buddy.

I ask Mommy what more signs say. She reads the words for me. Like "No Turn on Red." "Village Deli." "Nails and Things." There are words all over the place. That's what.

"Are you worried about reading, Nat?" Mommy asks.

"No," I answer. On account of I am worried about NOT reading.

But she looks at me like I said, *Yes, I am worried.* And that makes me think that my mom can read signs in my head. On account of those signs would be saying, "Natalie can't read!" And "Nat is too worried about it."

"Know what I think?" Mommy says. "I think you should try out those new school shoes right now."

I think this is a super good idea. I kick off my old shoes. I put on my new shoes. There are words on this shoe box. But I'm so thumpy-hearted about my new shoes that I don't even care.

Mommy parks Buddy in two spots. Somebody honks. Mommy is right. I don't think the honk is for Jesus.

We walk into the HyKlas through doors that *swish* open all by themselves. My new shoes go *squeak, squeak, squeak*.

Mommy takes a big silver shopping cart. I take a little yellow one.

Then Mommy gives me the rules. "Stay close. Okay, Nat? Don't forget. We don't *need* anything, do we? We may *want* some things, and we can talk about that. But we don't *need* anything."

"Why did we come here then?" I ask. On account of I could be home playing with my school stuff.

Mommy makes her balloon noise way better than Brianna did. "Just be good," she says. She pushes her cart to the first grocery-store street that goes by the name of Aisle One.

I hate that grocery street. There's nothing but yucky meats down that place. I skip to the next one.

Squeak, squeak squeak! go my brand-new school shoes.

Right away I see three things I need.

I very much love marshmallows. I plop a bag of those white fluffs into my yellow cart. Plus gum. Plus more gum. This is a really great grocery street.

I am almost turning to the next grocery street, when *pow!* My yellow cart crashes into another yellow cart.

"Hey! Watch out where you're going!" somebody yells.

I don't even have to look to see that somebody. On account of that somebody's voice goes with Sasha. Sasha is in my Sunday school class. Plus also, she was in my day care and my preschool. And she is sometimes a not-very-nice girl. That's what.

"*You* watch out too, Sasha," I say. I stare at her yellow cart. It is filled up with candy and chips and cookies.

A not-so-nice boy who goes by the name of Peter walks by with his mom. He is pushing a yellow cart.

And it's filled up with hot dogs. He makes a not-nice face at me.

"I need to get something from the bakery," says Peter's mom.

I think about telling her that nobody *needs* stuff from there.

She kisses Peter's head, and he tugs away. "You visit with your friends," says his mom. "I'll be right back."

Peter smiles at Sasha. "Wow! You've got cool stuff in your basket."

"My mother is taking snacks for the first week of kindergarten," Sasha says. "She's a volunteer helper." She says this like her mother is better than my mother.

I would like to dump her yellow cart out. That's what.

Peter makes a yucky face when he looks at my cart. "Who'd you get that junk for?" he asks.

But before I can answer, Sasha does. "Natalie probably got it for Jason, her boyfriend." She giggles. But she's not a giggle box.

Peter laughs in a mean way. "Is Jason your boyfriend?"

"Jason is my best friend who is a boy," I explain. I want to go on and tell them that this is not the same thing as a boyfriend.

But that Sasha is faster talking than me. She says, "Jason *is* your boyfriend, Natalie."

"You don't know, Sasha!" I shout.

Only she is not listening to me. She is mean giggling.

"Jason and Natalie sitting in a tree . . ." Peter sings this.

It makes me really aggravated. "Stop it!" I shout.

34

Even though I like sitting in a tree with my bestest friend who is a boy, Jason, and my bestest friend who is a girl, Laurie.

"Where's your *boyfriend*?" Sasha asks. She asks it snotty. So I know she doesn't really care where Jason is.

"Jason is *not* my boyfriend," I explain. "He is my friend. And a boy."

"So he's your *boyfriend*!" Peter laughs.

Then Sasha laughs.

"Is not!" I shout at that lying Peter.

"Is so!" he shouts back.

Then Sasha and Peter both start singing that stupid-head song about Jason and me in that tree.

I hate that song. That's what.

My hands squeeze the holding part of my yellow cart. "You better stop," I warn them.

"Natalie and Jason . . .," Sasha sings.

"Sitting in a tree," Peter sings.

"I mean it!" My eyes are lines, so I just see parts of those two guys. "Stop singing!"

Peter shouts back, "Make me!" He rams his cart into my cart. Then he takes off running.

And my very fast shoes take off after him.

Chapter 6

Shopping Cart Olympics

Peter runs down the grocery-store street, yelling, "I am Peter the Great! Nobody can catch me!"

I push my cart after him. "You are Peter the Not-So-Great!" I shout back. My feet are chasing. My shoes squeak faster and faster.

Peter runs up the grocery street just as my mom comes around the corner.

I stop running. But this is a hard thing on account of my new shoes are *so* fast.

"Natalie?" Mommy stares into my cart. "Do we really need these snacks?"

Sasha walks by us with her full shopping cart. She makes a frowny face at my cart. "Natalie really doesn't need snacks," she says. "My mother and I are bringing the kindergarten snacks."

Mommy and I put back all the stuff in my cart. Then we get different stuff for packing my kindergarten lunches. Like peanut butter and jelly and bread. And fruit. Plus also, cookies if I eat a fruit.

"Rats!" Mommy says. "I forgot milk. I'll go back.

Natalie, meet me at the checkout counter. Right there, okay?" She points all the way to the rows of checker-outers.

I watch her go. Then I walk toward the checking-out place. My shoes *squeak, squeak, squeak-squeak*. Faster and faster. These are very fast shoes.

One time, my daddy and I watched fast runners on TV in a world show that goes by the name of Olympics. And right now I have a picture of those guys in my head. Only I also see me with them. I am wearing a red-and-white-and-blue outfit just like the American team people. Only mine is also purple. On my back, in purple sparkly, is the number 24.

Inside my head an announcement is going off. And it sounds like this:

The whole wide world has come to the HyKlas Sports Place to see the amazing race that goes by the name of the Shopping Cart Olympics.

Every country from every world picked out their very fastest running person with the fastest new shoes. And America did not choose Peter. On account of he's too slow. And Sasha didn't even get to come and watch this show. That's what.

America picked out Natalie 24!

I can hear people cheering inside of my head when

they say "Natalie 24." This makes my heart all jumpy-thumpy.

My feet feel twitchy in my new shoes.

I push my shopping cart to the beginning of this grocery-store street.

Natalie 24 rolls her shopping cart to the starting line for the Shopping Cart Olympics. Her costume is the prettiest with purple in it. Her whole entire kindergarten class is cheering her on.

On your mark!

Get set!

Go!

When my head hears "Go!" my feet go. Very fast. My two feet run faster and faster. Only, one of my purple stripy shoes goes so fast, it flies off of my foot.

Natalie 24 is STILL running! She has one shoe on and one shoe off now, but she keeps on. For America! For kindergarten!

The Shopping Cart Olympics is halfway over. I know this 'cause of the cereal. Pancake boxes are behind me. Only cereal boxes are still in this grocery street aisle.

At the end of the aisle I see something surprising. A boy with a white apron is building a house out of cereal boxes.

Natalie 24 is getting really close to the finishing line for the first ever Shopping Cart Olympics! All of the watching people, and especially the kindergarteners, are jumping up and down and yelling, "Go, Natalie! Go, Natalie 24!"

I push my cart very much harder.

My one shoe goes *Squeak! Squeak! Squeak!*

With a giant burst of fast, I, Natalie 24, shove my cart across the finish line.

And into the cereal house.

That cereal house goes one way.

Then the other way.

A box tumbles off the very top.

Then all the cereals come crashing down.

When I open my eyes, the first person I see is Sasha. And she is mean giggling.

Sasha points to a sign at the front of the store. I peek out from under cereal boxes and look at that sign. I know those letters on there. But I don't know what words they're making.

"Natalie, see that?" Sasha asks. "It says, Don't Run! Can't you read?"

Chapter 7

The Kindie-Garden Plan

On Saturday before kindie-garden, I call a big plan with my bestest friend who is a girl and my bestest friend who is a boy. The sun is shiny hot. So we do our big plan in my back-yard.

Jason runs around like a monkey. He is a very good monkey. Only monkeys are hard to talk to and make a kindie-garden plan with.

"Jason, come back so we can talk!" Laurie shouts. Laurie and I are sitting under the biggest tree in my yard. This tree goes by the name of Frank. I named that tree myself.

Jason runs at us. Only now he is more like an ape than a monkey. "Grrrr!"

This turns Laurie and me into giggle boxes.

Jason doesn't slow himself down. He runs right into Frank. Then he climbs to the branch above Laurie and me.

This makes me think about Peter and Sasha singing about Jason and me in the tree. That stops me from being a giggle box.

"We really need a plan for kindie-garden," I say. I look up at Jason's feet hanging from Frank. "Jason, can you read?"

"Reading is for girls!" Jason shouts.

"No it isn't," Laurie says. "I mean, it is. But it's for boys too."

"Yeah," Jason admits. "But not for monkeys!" He makes a monkey sound.

"I mean it, Jason," I say. "I don't know if I want to go to kindie-garden." And this makes me kinda chokey to say.

"Me too," Laurie says very much soft.

Jason stops being a monkey. But he stays up in the tree. "How come?"

"What if everybody in kindie-garden can read except us?" I ask. "And Sasha and Peter and everybody make fun of us?"

"Yeah," Laurie agrees. Her voice is shaky.

Jason kicks Frank the Tree. "Then . . .," he shouts, "I will make them all wear weirdo funny glasses so they can't see the words and read. And *we* will laugh too!"

That makes Laurie have a smiley face.

But I have been thinking of other "ifs" too. "What if I get lost and can't find my classroom again?"

Laurie gets big in her eyes. On account of I don't think she thought about that one.

Jason grabs the branch above him and swings himself. "Then I will round up the posse. I will be the sheriff. And we won't stop looking until we find you, Nat!"

I try very hard to give my friend Jason a smiley face 'cause he would look for me with his posse. But my head is already thinking about another one of the "ifs."

"What if we have to color, and —?" I begin.

Only Laurie says, "I *love* to color. Sarah says we get to color a lot in kindergarten." Laurie is kinda smiley-faced about this. On account of she can color really good. And her color stays in between those lines, which mine does not.

"But what if I goof up and color red way out of the lines?" I ask. "And I get in trouble and get laughed at all over the place?"

Jason stops swinging on Frank's branch and plops back sitting down. "Then I will run all over the room and bump everybody's arm so they'll be outside of the lines too."

"Thanks, Jason," I say. And I really mean this. He is the bestest friend who is a boy in the whole world.

Percy, my fluffy white cat, sneaks over. But he doesn't love Jason, so he sneaks away.

And just that fast, I have another "if." "What if we eat lunch, and they only have a gazillion broccolis piled up?"

"Then I will sneak out of that place and get us hamburgers! And fries! And hot dogs!" Jason yells.

Laurie is pulling up some of the grass we're sitting on. "Nat, our moms bought us lunch boxes. We're packing our own lunches."

This is a true thing.

"Hey!" Jason shouts. "We get recess!"

"Yeah!" Laurie shouts. "They've got swings, Nat."

I want to be shouty like my friends. But I still don't feel shouty. "What if other kids hog the swings? Then what?" I can see Peter and Sasha doing that hogging.

"Then I will swoop down," Jason shouts as he jumps out of Frank the Tree, "and put spiders on those swings! And nobody but you and Laurie can sit there!"

Laurie giggles.

"But what if we're swinging and recess gets over and we don't know about it until it's too late?" I am seeing all of this happen inside my head. "And we bang and bang on the door because school is locked up and we can't get in?"

"I'll drive my helicopter to school," Jason promises. "And I will drop a ladder down the school chimney so you can climb back into school!"

Laurie is a giggle box. "Plus, Sarah says the teacher blows a whistle when recess is over."

Only I left the biggest "if" until last, on account of I don't even like to think about this one. That's what.

We are quiet for a minute. I think my face must be frowny 'cause my bestest friends are big in their eyes looking at me.

"What's wrong, Nat?" Laurie asks.

Even thinking this makes my neck so chokey that I have to swallow to get words out. "What if . . . ?" I swallow again. "What if the teacher doesn't know I go by the name of Natalie 24? And what if she calls me Natalie Elizabeth? And kids like Peter and not-so-nice Sasha laugh 'cause the teacher calls me Elizabeth?"

Nobody answers this for a minute. A dog barks from across the road. Somebody's TV laughs too loud. The sun winks on and off on account of a bunch of clouds are in the sky to hide behind.

Finally Jason yells, "Then I will make our teacher write on the board twenty-four times: *Natalie 24! Natalie 24!*" And Jason keeps yelling this until Laurie yells it too.

My face can't help being a little smiley at my bestest friends when they yell this.

And before I know it, I am a giggle box. That's what.

And I am thinking that maybe the first day of kindergarten will be just fine, so long as I got Jason and Laurie there with me.

Chapter 8

The Day before Kindergarten

"Mommy," I say, trying not to let it sound like whining. My mommy hates whining. "Why can't I wear my new shoes to Sunday school? It's a school too, you know."

We are standing at my front door and trying to go to Sunday school and church. This can be a harder thing than you think it is.

"It's raining, Natalie," Mommy answers. She stuffs my arms into my raincoat that isn't purple. "You want your new shoes to get ruined before you even get to wear them to kindergarten?"

"Besides," Daddy says, "your new shoes are way too fast for church."

This might could be a true thing. They don't like fast running in our church. I sit on the floor and stick out my feet. Mommy puts one old shoe on me. Daddy puts one old shoe on my other foot. Only it won't go. They look up at each other. Then they switch shoes and try again. This time it works.

We do much hurrying to get to church. But when

I get to my Sunday school classroom, most kids are already there and sounding like bumbly bees.

"I saved you a seat, Nat!" shouts my bestest friend, Laurie. She is the best seat saver in the whole world.

I wave and run to that saved seat. "Laurie, will you save me a seat in kindergarten tomorrow?" I ask.

Before Laurie can say yes, Sasha turns around from her seat on the very front row. She sticks in her nose where there's not her business. "Laurie can't save you a seat in kindergarten, Natalie. They have signed seats. Your name will already be on one. Probably in alphabet order." She turns back around.

I make a frowny face at that Sasha. Only she is already too turned around to see it.

"Let's ask Sarah if Sasha is lying or truthing," I

whisper to Laurie.

"Sarah had to stay home from church," Laurie says. "She's sick. So's Bri."

I hope very hard that Sasha is lying.

Our Sunday school teacher starts talking. She is a very good teacher about God. Only we are kinda bumbly bees still.

I look around for my bestest friend who is a boy. "Where's Jason?" I ask Laurie. 'Cause I don't see that boy in here.

Laurie shrugs up her shoulders in the I-don't-know way.

This is a weird thing on account of Jason is always in Sunday school. Plus also, you always know where he is when he's anywhere near you.

"I know you must be excited about school starting tomorrow," Mrs. Palmer says. She is kind of shouty. But we are still kind of like bumbly bees. "So let's begin by praying for you and the start of school."

I think this is a very good idea.

"Father, thank you for all of these children," Mrs. Palmer begins.

I close my eyes so my Sunday school teacher can talk to God without me looking. She is closing her eyes too. But I have to peek to see this part.

And that's how I see something else. Behind Mrs. Palmer is a marker board. And on that board are words. Many words.

I can't stop staring at those words. I know one of them — *Jesus*. But not those others on account of I can't read.

"Amen," Mrs. Palmer says loud.

I missed almost that whole entire prayer. So I do my own. Only I keep the words inside and my eyes open. And it works this way too. *God, help me make it through kindergarten. Make me read. And thanks a gazillion for my bestest friend Laurie and my bestest friend who*  *is a boy but not my boyfriend and goes by the name of Jason. Thanks that Jason will bump arms of kids coloring inside the lines if they make fun of me. And thanks that Jason will round up a posse if I get lost. And thanks that Jason will make kids wear funny glasses if they read so good that they make fun of me for not.*

Chapter 9

A Gazillion Names

I say "Amen" after that open-eye prayer. I am watching Mrs. Palmer. She picks up an eraser and moves to the marker board.

"Wait!" I shout. "Don't!"

Mrs. Palmer turns around. She is holding that eraser up like a music leader. "What's wrong, Natalie?"

"Please don't erase those words!" I shout. "What do they say?"

Mrs. Palmer frowns at the marker board like she's never seen one before. "Well, I think this must be left over from Pastor's Bible study last night. They're studying the names of Jesus."

"Huh?" I ask. 'Cause even I know that one. "His name's Jesus. That's what. So how come our pastor has to teach that? And how come there are so many of those names?"

Mrs. Palmer puts down her eraser. "You know, Natalie, that's a great question. I think we'll take a look before we start our own lesson."

I feel good about asking a good question. I will

remember this question for kindergarten if I need a good question one day.

Mrs. Palmer moves to the marker board. "There are several names for the Son of God," she says. She points to the one with a big *J*. "I think we all know this one, right? What's it say, class?"

"Jesus!" we yell.

"And that one says Christ, like in Christmas," Sasha says.

Mrs. Palmer points to that word. "Yes. And Son of God, Son of Man, Messiah, Rabbi or Teacher, Prince of Peace, Wonderful Counselor, Almighty God, Savior." She moves down the list, reading those names. "Advocate, Anointed One, Mediator, Redeemer, High Priest."

At the very end of that list are two letters. I know one letter, and it goes by the name of A. But the other letter looks weird, like a horseshoe. "What are those for?" I ask. "Those letters all by themselves?"

"I almost missed those, didn't I?" Mrs. Palmer admits. "You know the letter A, I'll bet. This one is called Omega. *A* is the first letter in our own alphabet and in the Greek alphabet. But in the Greek alphabet—and the New Testament was written in Greek —Omega is the last letter. Like our letter Z."

She writes a big *Z* on the board. "Alpha and Omega, the first letter and last letter, meaning the beginning and the end. In Revelation, that's another name for God and Jesus. I think it's a good one. Nothing's left out between the first and the last, right?"

I stare at those two letters. In my head, I hum the ABC song and think of the letters that go with it. I know that song really good. And I know those real letters that go "L, M, N, O, P." When I was a little kid, my daddy made up the words that go there: "H-I-J-K-Micky Mantle, please."

Mrs. Palmer points to the name that has *I* starting it.

"Anyone recognize this name for Jesus?" she asks.

Not even Sasha answers. So Mrs. Palmer does. "Immanuel. That means 'God with us.' God is with us at all times."

"Did anybody really call Jesus Immanuel?" I ask. On account of I think kids would make fun of that name.

"Of course," Mrs. Palmer says. "But mostly people called him Joshua, or Jesus."

"I think Jesus made the right choice going with Jesus," I say. And I am thinking about me going by Natalie 24 instead of Natalie Elizabeth. But I like that name Immanuel, with the thought built into it about Jesus always being around.

Then that makes me think about Jason— *not* being around. On account of I don't see him in my Sunday school room.

"Deshawn!" I shout. I have to shout 'cause he's sitting four rows away. He lives next door to Jason's mom and Jason. "Where's Jason?"

"Natalie?" says Mrs. Palmer. "May I help you with something so we can get on with our lesson for today?"

"Maybe," I answer. "Where's Jason?"

That not-so-nice boy who goes by the name of Peter the Not-So-Great raises his hand. "*I* know!" he shouts.

"Jason's with his dad because his parents are divorced."

"All right then," Mrs. Palmer says. She says this with a smiley face. But I don't think she likes Peter telling the world about Jason's parents.

"They have to split Jason up." Peter keeps going. "His mom gets him most of the time. And his dad moved to Florida and gets Jason for like a week at a time."

"That's enough, Peter," Mrs. Palmer says. She turns to the board with all of Jesus' names on it and starts to erase. "Shall we get back to the lesson now?"

Only Peter won't let her. "Jason is with his dad for a whole week this time, and he didn't even know he was going there. But my dad says Jason's dad is taking him to Disneyland so he won't feel bad about missing the first week of school. Mom says Jason's dad is a Disneyland Dad."

"Wait a minute," I say. For the first time, I turn around so I can see Peter. 'Cause I want to see him take it back—what he just said about Jason. "Jason wouldn't miss school."

"Jason, your boyfriend . . . ," Peter begins.

Only I don't even care that some kids are giggling at that boyfriend word. I want Peter to keep going.

"Jason," Peter goes on, "is going to Disneyland all

56

week instead of going to kindergarten like he should."

"But—but—" Words are having trouble getting out of the chokey part of my neck. My head is fuzzy. My heart is thumpy. Who else is going to round up the posse if I get lost? Or bump everybody's arms and make them go out of the lines if they make fun of me coloring? Or bring hamburgers if we only get broccoli? Or spiders if we can't get a swing?

Or, if I'm the only one who can't read words, who's going to bring crazy glasses for the reading kids?

Jason *has* to go to kindergarten, or I'm not going either. That's what.

Chapter 10

Kindergarten Morning

"I don't think I should go to kindergarten until Jason gets back," I tell Mommy. I still have on my favorite jammies with 24 on the back, which is the name of my favorite number.

"Don't be silly, Nat," Mommy says, sitting down on my bed with me. "You can't miss your first day of kindergarten. Hop to it, sleepyhead."

Percy hops off my bed. I am not a sleepyhead. I have been awake a very long time. Only I just didn't get up yet. Half of me kinda wants to hop out of bed like

Percy and get to that kindergarten place and be a kindergarten girl. Only the other half of me wants to pull my covers up over my head.

"Well, I'd hate to drive only Laurie to kindergarten all by herself," Mommy says.

This doesn't make sense. "Laurie's mom drives all of her kids to school herself," I tell her.

Mommy shakes her head. "Not this morning. Sarah and Brianna are both too sick to go to school. So I offered to drive Laurie to —"

"To kindergarten!" I say. And I hop out of bed faster than my cat, Percy. "With me!"

"Yep," Mommy says. "So you better get on your first-day-of-kindergarten clothes. I'm scrambling eggs for breakfast."

My heart is starting to be thumpy in the good way. My bestest friend, Laurie, and I are driving to kinder-garten together in Buddy.

Mommy and I set out my clothes the night before. And those clothes are still there on my chair. I put on new everything. First, I put on my new speedy shoes.

Then I pull on my new skirt that isn't jeans. I think maybe Laurie is pulling on *her* skirt that isn't jeans. And we are twin-skirt girls. Then I put on my new top that is like Laurie's, except purple.

Percy is watching me.

"Percy," I tell him, "today, Laurie and I are twin kindergarten girls. That's what."

When I walk out to the kitchen, my heart is still thumpy.

Daddy is sitting at the breakfast table. He puts down his newspaper and gets big in his eyes. "Wow! Natalie 24, you look just like a kindergarten girl!"

"I *am* a kindergarten girl, Daddy!" I shout. "Laurie and I are kindergarten twin girls."

My mom makes a sniffy noise. She is very red in her eyes. "Oh, Natalie," she says. "You're going to kindergarten." She wipes her eyes with the back of her hand. "You're such a big girl now. I remember the day you were born. And now you're going to school. Before

I know it, you'll be in high school. And college. And married." She sniffs.

"Married?" I can't tell if she's teasing me, like Peter did about a boyfriend.

"Your daddy and I met in kindergarten," Mommy says. "He swept me right off my feet."

This is new news to me. About the sweeping part. I will stay away from any boy with a broom in the whole entire school.

Daddy reaches across the breakfast table and squeezes Mommy's arm. "Nat, you may have to look out for your mother this morning. I'm really sorry I can't go with you. But I'll get fired if I go in to work late. Take care of your mom for me."

Mommy waves a napkin at him. "Bill, stop it." She brings the napkin to her eyes 'cause she's got tears in there. "I'm just so happy. And proud of Natalie."

"'Cause I'm a kindergarten girl?" I ask.

"Exactly," Daddy says.

"I'll get the camera!" Mommy shouts. She runs and gets her camera and takes a gazillion pictures of me.

Daddy gives me a longer-than-usual, squishy hug. "Now go knock their socks off, kindergarten girl!"

Mommy and I only have to drive Buddy a little bit to get Laurie, 'cause she lives on our very own street.

"This is a good idea to drive Laurie to kindergarten," I say.

"I feel sorry for Brianna and Sarah," Mommy says. "I think they have the flu."

A school bus drives right by us. It's filled with kids. "I wish we lived far away from school so I could ride a bus." I whisper this so I don't hurt Buddy's feelings.

"Maybe you'll make a new friend today who lives in the country, Nat," Mommy says. "And if you go home with your new friend someday, then you could ride the bus."

"I don't need a new friend," I say. "I have Laurie." But I am thinking about Laurie and me making a new friend together and both of us riding on a school bus to the country.

Mommy pulls Buddy into Laurie's driveway. "I'll get Laurie!" I shout.

I'm so excited that I can't unpop my seat belt. Mommy has to help. I run up the driveway and start to knock on Laurie's door.

Only before I can, the door opens.

It's not Laurie. It's just Laurie's mom standing there. "Oh, Natalie. I'm sorry. I tried to call you, but you'd already left. Your mom doesn't have her cell on."

"That's okay," I say. "Where's Laurie?"

"That's just it, honey," she says. "Laurie's sick. I think she caught a virus from her sisters. *Achoo!*" She sneezes loud. "You better step back, Natalie. I think I'm coming down with this thing too."

"But Laurie can't NOT go to school!" I shout.

"She's in bed, honey," she says. "Believe me, she's more upset about this than you are. You'll have to call her after school and tell her all about it, okay?"

"But we're supposed to be kindergarten twins." My neck is so chokey that my eyes hurt.

Laurie's mom sneezes again and steps back inside her house. "Natalie, you have a great day, hear? Call us." She covers her mouth with her arm and sneezes again. Then she waves at Buddy and closes the door.

I walk back to Buddy and get in. My neck is burny.

Mommy is staring at me. "Nat, did Laurie catch that flu bug too?"

I shake my head in the yes way. Then I look up at my mom and tell her, "Now I really and for true can't go to that kindergarten place."

And this feels like a true thing.

Chapter 11

Not Here

"No, Mommy! Turn Buddy around!" I shout. She is still driving toward that kindergarten place.

"Natalie, we're going to be late to your first day of kindergarten if you keep this up," she says, without turning Buddy around.

"But Jason won't be there. And Laurie won't be there." I tell her in case she forgot that part.

"I'm sorry about that, honey. But it doesn't matter. You'll still have a great day. Come on, now. You've been to preschool when Laurie was on vacation."

"Not *real* school. Not all day. Not kindergarten! Why do *I* have to go to school if Laurie and Jason don't?"

Mommy makes her balloon noise. "Everybody goes to school, Natalie. Even Jesus went to school when he was your age."

This is new news to me. Even Jesus had to go to school? I sit without arguing on account of I'm all out of arguing.

On the side of my school is a big parking lot. We leave Buddy there with a gazillion cars. Then we walk up the sidewalk.

In front of me, a kid in jeans and a pink shirt is hippy-hopping. She is so smiley-faced. And this is a funny thing on account of her mom is crying.

Two big boys run in front of us. One has a basket-ball. They're laughing their heads off.

"Matt!" one yells. "Heads up!" He throws the ball at the other kid.

We walk by medium-sized girls blocking the side-walk. They are squealing in a cheerleading way, like they're so happy to see each other.

A bus stops, and the doors swoosh open. Bus kids come out. Some are little and might could be going to kindergarten. One girl is very big in her eyes, even though her eyes are longer than mine, like a girl in my preschool who goes by the name of Lena and comes from a country called China.

Behind her is a girl with red hair. I wave to her on account of she was in my Mommy's Day Out.

Her name is Rory. She waves back.

"Hey, Kelly!" another mommy shouts to mine.

"Hi, Megan!" Mommy shouts back. "Big day, huh?" Mommy leans down to me. "Her son is in the other kindergarten class, I think. Samuel."

I know Samuel. He's pretty nice. I would like that kid to be in *my* class.

Three mommies come out of the front door we're walking in. They're laughing and looking like cheer-leading mommies.

"Freedom!" one shouts. She skips down the steps.

"Let's go shopping!" says the other one. She jumps all three steps and lands on the sidewalk.

"I'm already late for work," says the third mom.

My mom doesn't look like any of those cheerlead-ing moms. She is red in her eyes.

"Natalie," she says, "this is it, honey." She makes her mouth smiley. But not her eyes.

We are holding hands. I don't let go. She doesn't let go.

Then I feel her fingers slipping out of mine. I let them slip. Only I can still feel my mom's fingers. And they're not even there.

"You can come," I say. I don't know if this is a for-true thing or not.

"Maybe another day," Mommy says.

"Coming through!" Sasha pushes right in between my mom and me.

My classroom is the second one down the hall. I watch Sasha go right into that room.

"Bye, Nat." Mommy kisses my head. "I'll be right here to pick you up as soon as school is over." Her voice sounds funny. Then she turns and walks away.

I watch the back of my mommy getting farther and farther away. Then another bus dumps off a bunch of noisy kids. And I can't see my mommy anymore.

On account of she is not here.

And Jason is not here.

And Laurie is not here.

And only I am here.

That's what.

Chapter 12

Roll Call

I walk into my classroom and stop. I know some of these kids. Like Rory with the red hair. And Bethany.

And Peter. And Sasha.

Only nobody waves at me.

Nobody saved me a seat.

"Hello, Natalie," Miss Hines, our teacher, says. She bends down so I see her face. It is a smiley face with black hair around it and brown eyes in it. "I'm so happy to welcome you to your first day of kindergarten!" she says.

"Thanks," I say. Only I'm also seeing other stuff. Like a cage with a fuzzy animal in there.

And rows of desks.

And kids putting their backpacks on hooks.

And a big marker board.

Over the marker board, there are letters up there. Big letters, with little letters next to them. I know those big letters by name. And most of the little letters. But not words when the letters go together. On account of I can't read.

"Why don't you come over and meet Anna?" says the teacher, who goes by the name of Miss Hines. "Your desks are next to each other. So are your cubbies. That's where you can hang your coat and store your backpack."

I want to say something, but I don't know what.

So I just follow our teacher over to a row of shelves. And there is that girl who looks like Lena from China. She has black hair and is even littler than me. I know this must be the girl who goes by the name of Anna.

Miss Hines tells us who we are. "Anna, this is Natalie. Natalie, this is Anna."

"Hi," Anna says very soft. "This is my first day of kindergarten."

"Me too," I tell her.

I'm not crazy about leaving my new purple backpack in my cubby. A cubby turns out to be just a big hole out of wood. And I know that's my name on there. But I still don't want to leave my backpack. So I put it back on my back, where it's safe.

"I like your shoes," Anna says.

I think this is a very nice thing to say. So I say the same thing. "I like *your* shoes."

"Anna, come over and see this hamster!" A girl with blonde braids grabs Anna by the arm and pulls her to the cage.

I would like to see that fuzzy hamster in that cage. Only nobody pulls *my* arm to show me that thing.

I am standing all by myself. And it feels lonely. So I go and sit in one of the desks.

"That's not *your* desk," Sasha says.

I stop sitting down and look at the name on the desk. I don't know what the name says. But I know it isn't my name. There's no *N* in that whole name.

"Yours is back there," Sasha says. She runs off.

"Did you find your desk?" Miss Hines asks. She doesn't wait for me to answer. She shows me to a desk on the end and in the back. And there is my name on that desk.

"Will everyone please find your desk?" Miss Hines asks. "Anyone need help?"

Two girls raise their hands. One is kinda crying. She has long black hair that she could sit on. And she is standing behind our teacher.

I don't think our teacher sees the long-haired girl's hand. So I stand up and wave at the girl. "Hey! Our teacher has a desk with your name on it!" I say this very loud, on account of I am in the way back.

A bunch of kids turn and look at me. Sasha is one of those kids. Plus also, she is frowny-faced.

I slide back down in my desk.

But our teacher turns around and sees that kid with the long hair. And guess what? She walks that kid to the next backest row. And that kid's desk is right in front of mine. That's what.

When that kid sits down, she lifts up her long black hair so she won't sit on it. I think she gives me a tiny smiley face before she turns herself around.

Pretty soon, we are all in our desks. Only it wasn't easy.

"Miss Hines?" Sasha asks. "What if we don't like our desk? Can we trade for one on the front row?" Her desk is on row two.

"Let's all get used to these for today, Sasha. Okay?" Miss Hines asks back.

Miss Hines moves to the front of the room and stands in the front of her desk. Her desk is a gazillion times bigger than our desks. She is the teacher.

"Welcome to kindergarten!" she says.

Miss Hines is a very good kindergarten cheerleader. She tells us about our school.

And our cubbies.

And how we'll go to the washroom and take turns.

And the drinking fountains.

And how we can go other times if we raise our hands.

And how everything is so much fun.

Then she starts talking about the rules for school. It turns out there are many rules in this place.

Like no running.

And no poking.

And no chewing gum.

And no taking other kids' stuff.

And always raising our hands to ask anything.

Peter raises his hand.

"Yes, Peter," Miss Hines says.

"How many more rules are there?" he asks.

Sasha laughs.

"That's about it," Miss Hines says.

I'm wondering if the school people know God made up all of *his* rules into only just ten.

"So," Miss Hines says, "let's start the day with roll call." She picks up a notebook from her desk. "When I call your name, please raise your hand and answer 'Present' or 'Here.'"

"Michael Adams?" she calls.

"Present here!" yells Michael Adams.

"That's great," Miss Hines says. "You can just say one or the other, though. 'Present' or 'Here.' Now, do you want us to call you Michael or Mike?"

"Michael," he answers. He says this like Miss Hines is crazy for thinking he could ever be a Mike.

Miss Hines keeps calling out names. When she gets to Peter, he says, "Present. And you can call me Peter the Great!"

I try to pay attention to other names. But my stomach is all twitchy waiting for my name.

"Natalie Elizabeth?" Miss Hines says.

My heart is very thumpy. Maybe there is another Natalie in this class. Maybe there is a Natalie who likes that name Elizabeth.

"Natalie Elizabeth?" Miss Hines says again, more loud.

I stare at my desk. It is shiny and white speckly.

"Natalie Elizabeth?" Miss Hines stares right at me. "Just say 'Here.'"

I am just Natalie, I want to say. *I am Natalie 24*, I want to shout.

I want Jason to be here and make our teacher write this on the marker board twenty-four times.

Peter turns around and makes a frowny face at me. "Hey! Natalie Lizard Breath! She's calling your name."

Chapter 13

Kindergarten Twins!

"Natalie?" Miss Hines takes off her glasses. She doesn't sound aggravated. "Is there something else you want us to call you? That's okay if there is. Just tell us."

I am sitting all alone.

I don't have my bestest friends who are a boy and a girl.

I have never felt so much alone as I am right now.

I am hoping my words will make it past that lumpy in my neck. "My name is Natalie 24," I say. Only I say this so soft that maybe only I can hear it.

"What was that?" Miss Hines asks. She puts her glasses back on, like that will make her hear better.

I take in air in a giant breath. Then I let it out and say really loud, "Natalie 24!"

Sasha turns around frowny-faced at me. "That's a number, not a name." She turns back around at our teacher and says, "Her name is too Natalie Elizabeth. She can't have a different name."

Only Sasha is wrong. Even Jesus had more names than just the one.

So I say so to Sasha, "I can too have more names. And Natalie 24 is it. That's what."

All of a sudden I am really glad that Jesus had other names. I think of that other name for Jesus, Immanuel. I love that name. On account of it means that Jesus is with us.

With me.

Even here.

Even now.

So maybe I'm not so much alone as I think I am.

"Natalie 24 it is," says Miss Hines.

I really like this teacher.

She goes on to call other names. Like Farah for the girl with long black hair in front of me. And Griffin, who says his name is Griff.

I lean back in my desk. But I keep thinking about

Jesus being here too. With me. And maybe how he could be my kindergarten twin until Laurie gets back.

"I wish I had a number in my name," whispers Anna, the girl in the next desk.

"I like your name," I say.

When we're all done saying that we're here, Miss Hines lets us sit on the floor, on a soft blue rug. She reads us a story about a little girl's first day of kindergarten. In that story, there's a classroom pet, like ours.

One kid, Erika, raises her hand for the bathroom. Then three more kids raise their hands. Then a little boy dances in a circle and says he's got to go.

So we get a washroom break. And that is more fun than you think it is.

When we're back in our room, Miss Hines helps us find the right desks again.

Then she says, "I thought it might be fun to make your parents a first-day-of-kindergarten card!" She says this like a cheerleading teacher.

My heart goes thumpy. I would *love* to take home a card for my mommy and daddy.

Miss Hines has the red-haired girl named Rory and the boy named Griff give us heavy white paper that looks like a card with a flower drawn on it.

"Get out your crayons or markers," Miss Hines

says. "You can color the flower on the front of your card in any way you choose."

I hate coloring.

Anna leans over to me and whispers, "I love to color. Don't you?"

I shake my head in the no way. "But my bestest friend, Laurie, who is not here, loves to color."

Other kids are coloring like crazy.

I peek at the long-haired girl in front of me. She is a very good colorer.

I take a very long time getting my colors out of my purple backpack. Then I put those crayons back. And I take out my brand-new markers.

When I open the box, there is the purple marker. Right in the middle.

"Better get started, Natalie," says Miss Hines. She is standing beside me, and I didn't even know that. But she isn't mean about it.

When she goes away, I take out my new purple marker. I wonder if I can smell that purpley. So I put my nose very close to that marker. It does smell purpley.

I stare at the white card. It would look so pretty if that flower got all purple.

I put my purple marker on one of the flowery parts of the flower. And I color.

A little bit of purpley goes outside that flower part. Only not so bad.

I do that again with another flower part. It's not so bad too.

I stare at those purple flower parts. I can smell the purpley in my marker. And I wonder what purpley tastes like.

I am wondering. And that purple marker is getting closer to my mouth. And closer.

And then that purple marker is inside my mouth.

Only not for very long. On account of that thing tastes horrible. That's what.

I go back to coloring my flower. I like doing this. I pretend Jesus, who goes by the name of Immanuel, is coloring a purple sky. And I am coloring purple flowers. And we are coloring up the world together.

But I think most kids are done. So I color faster. And faster.

When I stop, I look at my purpley flower. And my stomach feels twitchy in a not-good way. On account of that purple is out of the lines all over the place.

I want very much for Jason to be here. He could bump the other kids and make their flowers look like mine.

I think I'm the only one in all kindergarten to have so much color out of my lines.

I slap my hands on top of my flower card so nobody can see. I am a terrible colorer. That's what.

Only I'm still thinking about Jesus Immanuel being next to me. Coloring. And he is whispering inside my head: *"Great job, Natalie 24! You did your best. Plus, I love purple!"*

My neck starts being un-chokey, just thinking this—that Jesus loves purple. Even when the purpley is outside the lines.

"Yuck!" Sasha says this so loud we all look at her.

She is turned around and pointing. And she is pointing at me. "Look at Natalie! She's been sucking on her marker, Miss Hines."

I shake my head. "Have not!" I yell. On account of I did not suck on that purple yucky.

"Yeah, right," she says. And she laughs very mean.

Then other kids laugh.

And other kids wrinkle up their faces like they tasted that purpley too.

The long-haired girl in front of me points to her teeth. Only she's got nothing on there. She points again and nods at me.

And I get it.

"Natalie," Anna whispers, "you have purple teeth."

Chapter 14

Recess

Miss Hines sends all the rest of the kids to recess with the other kindergarten teacher. That teacher doesn't look mean like Brianna said she was.

"Natalie, we can get you washed up over here," Miss Hines says. She leads me to a sink.

"Maybe I should go home," I tell her. I have many reasons for this idea. "We have a sink there. And we have soap. And my mommy is a good scrubber. Plus also, Percy is missing me." I feel kinda chokey for Percy.

"Is Percy your little brother?" Miss Hines asks.

"Kinda. He's my cat," I say.

"I love cats," Miss Hines says.

I stand on a step and lean over the sink. This might could be a fun thing if I didn't have purpley all over me.

My teacher waters a paper towel and wipes it on my mouth. She rubs where my mustache would be if I had one of those things.

"Smile," she says. Then she goes for my teeth.

It tickles. I smile for real.

"I love washable markers," Miss Hines says.

"Me too," I agree. "Except for they don't taste good."

"Which is a great reason not to allow them into your mouth. Right?" She stares at me with this question.

I stare back. "Right."

Then we both go out to recess.

"Have fun, Natalie," Miss Hines says when we are out in the sunshine. But she has to run off 'cause red-headed Rory is crying for her.

There are kids of different sizes out here. Four girls from my class are sitting on the step and talking. This does not look like a fun thing.

A bunch of boys are throwing balls at each other.

And there are swings in this place.

"Natalie! I saved you a swing!" Anna hollers.

I cannot believe Anna did this. Now I know two seat savers. That's what!

"Coming!" I yell.

Anna and I swing and talk at the same time.

I keep watching the playground.

"Who are you looking for?" Anna asks.

"Nobody," I answer. "I just don't want to miss the ending of recess and get locked out of the school. Jason isn't here to get me back in."

"Who's Jason?" Anna asks. She is a really good swinging girl.

"Jason is my bestest friend who is a boy. And that's not the same thing as my boyfriend," I say quick.

Anna nods. She doesn't giggle.

So I tell her all about Jason and how he promised to get me into the school by dropping me from a helicopter through the chimney.

The mean kindergarten teacher who's not ours blows a whistle at us.

Kids run and line up to go back inside.

"Guess we won't need Jason's helicopter," Anna says.

"Guess we don't need the posse," I say.

When it's our turn to go to lunch, I walk to my cubby. And there's my lunch box. I think about my bestest friend, Laurie, not getting to use her lunch box today. And that makes me frowny. So I tell Jesus — on account of he's here — that it would be very nice if he could make Laurie all better, please.

Anna and most of the kids get into a line to pick up school lunches. So I have to stand in the cafeteria all alone. I hold my lunch box with both hands and look around. I wish Laurie could be here. And Jason.

There are big kids in here too. And they are full of noises.

I sit down at a table with only me. It feels like everybody is staring at me and saying, "Look! Nobody wants to sit by Natalie."

Only then I remember Immanuel. So I have my brain picture Jesus sitting down across from me. And this makes me not so much alone.

I open my lunch box and think Jesus must love peanut butter. In my head I say thanks for making that peanut buttery stuff when he made the world. Amen.

I look around and see that long-haired girl. She is standing like I was. All alone. Only she has a tray of food and not a lunch box.

A bigger boy bumps her, and her whole tray almost drops.

"Hey! Farah!" I remember that name on account of it sounds like "Sarah," only not. "Sit here!" I shout.

Farah gets almost smiley-faced at that. She heads toward me.

And another thing happens. Anna sits down next to me.

Then Farah sets her tray down across from my lunch box. She sits right in that seat where Jesus was.

And he doesn't even mind at all.

Chapter 15

Dancing with Letters

"Where do you live?" Anna asks Farah.

"In the country," Farah answers.

My brain wakes up. "In the country? Do you ride a school bus?"

Farah shakes her head in the yes way. "It was a long ride."

"You're so lucky!" I say. I remember what my mommy said about riding home with a friend in the country one day. On a school bus.

We eat our lunches, and I tell Farah and Anna all about my bestest friend, Laurie. On account of they have to be her friends too.

Anna and Farah and I are giggling so hard when lunch is over that we end up in the way back of the lunch crowd.

I don't want to be late. But you're not supposed to run in the halls. So I walk really fast. My legs are stiff. My arms reach back and up. My shoes are so fast, even walking.

"Hey! Slow down!" Sasha yells.

"You're not the boss of me, Sasha!" I shout back. 'Cause I am passing that slow girl. That's what.

"You're not fooling anybody by walking fast!" Sasha shouts behind me. "You can ruin your whole school that way!"

Only I get to my classroom that way. And I don't even ruin my school.

In the afternoon, our teacher reads us another story that is very funny. I try to get to know our classroom pet that goes by the name of Ham the Hamster. And I am starting to think that I kinda like this place that goes by the name of kindergarten.

Only then Miss Hines says, "Time to finish our first-day cards for our parents." She writes a word on the marker board while we watch her. "We'll be spending a lot of time becoming friends with the letters you see all around our classroom."

I look up and see those letters above the marker board: *Aa, Bb, Cc, Dd,* . . . Then I look at the word our teacher wrote.

I stare at those word letters again. They are lined up over the board. Marching. Laughing at me for not knowing them.

And I get kinda chokey.

"L-O-V-E," says Miss Hines. "Love."

I wish I could have known that word before she said it. I wonder if everybody in here could read that word, except me.

"I'd like each of you to copy those letters and then print your name. So your card will say 'Love,' and your name. But don't worry. I'm here to help. And we have two volunteer moms to help us too."

This is a true thing I didn't notice before. Two moms have shown up and are standing in the doorway. One of those moms has treats and belongs to Sasha.

We get to work. I try my hardest to write those letters. The mom who isn't Sasha's helps me make the *V* right-side up. And my teacher helps me make my name better.

They are very nice. Plus we get snacks.

But my letters aren't straight like the ones on the board.

I lean back in my desk and stare up at those marching letters and wonder if letters can really laugh at a kid.

Then I see something.

I stare at that first letter, *A*. Then I stare at that last letter, *Z*. My head still has a picture of a horseshoe in it, on account of the marker board in Sunday school.

First letter, last letter. In my mind, those names for Jesus come together. Immanuel. First and Last. That means he's here. And he's in those letters too! Plus also, in between them.

So those letters can't be scary. They might be marching. But I like marching. I could march with them! And if they're laughing, I can laugh too.

A bell rings.

I think our teacher says to go home. I think she says

that walkers should go stand here. And bus riders go there.

Only I am still staring at those letters. Then I stand up. I march to my cubby. I put on my purple backpack, and I do a twirl.

On account of I am dancing with those letters. That's what.

Chapter 16

What Kindergarten Learned on the First Day of Nat

As soon as I get home, I call my bestest friend who is a girl. And Laurie and I talk like chatterboxes.

"Now I'm afraid I'll really be behind in kindergarten," Laurie says, after I tell her everything about that place.

"No! That's one thing I learned at kindergarten!" I shout to the phone.

So I tell Laurie the best things I learned on kindergarten's first day of me. And these are the things:

1. Nobody's behind! We learn everything.
2. You don't ruin your school by walking fast. Only just running.
3. Don't stick your finger into a hamster cage.
4. Don't suck on a marker 'cause the color will come off on your teeth, and everybody will know you did it. Plus also, they don't taste that good.
5. You don't have to be alone in that place, on account of even though Jesus is God's Son, he still goes to kindergarten.

Check out the other books in the series—available now!

Natalie has big five-year-old dreams for her future. So big, that her heart gets thumpy with excitement. Nat uses her very own words to tell about her hopes, struggles, and adventures. This makes the That's Nat! series perfect for young readers just ready for chapter books.

Book 1: Natalie and the One-of-a-Kind Wonderful Day!

Book 2: Natalie Really Very Much Wants to Be a Star

Book 4: Natalie and the Downside-Up Birthday

Book 5: Natalie and the Bestest Friend Race

Book 6: Natalie Wants a Puppy

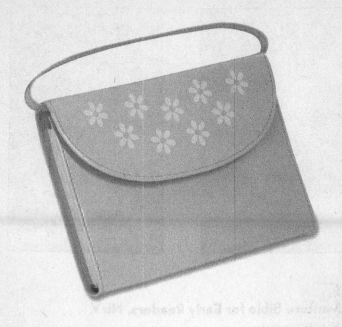

My Little Purse Bible
ISBN: 9780310822660

This is an adorable purse-like Bible cover that comes with a complete New Testament edition of the NIrV translation with Psalms and Proverbs. This is available for a limited time and perfect for the Easter Holiday.

Ad
ISE

No
Bib
wri
Kid
to

Th
fo
ISE

Bu
Bib
live
ne

Avail